SO-ASQ-859

Cerullo, Mary M.,
Sharks of the deep : a
shark photographer's se
[2015].
33305233084858
sa   04/15/15

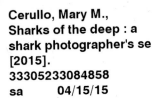

ark Expedition

SHARKS OF THE DEEP:
A SHARK PHOTOGRAPHER'S SEARCH FOR SHARKS AT THE BOTTOM OF THE SEA

by Mary M. Cerullo

Photographs by Jeffrey L. Rotman

Consultant: James Sulikowski, PhD
Marine Science Department, University of New England

COMPASS POINT BOOKS
a capstone imprint

Compass Point Books are published by Capstone,
1710 Roe Crest Drive, North Mankato, Minnesota 56003
www.capstonepub.com

Copyright © 2015 by Compass Point Books, a Capstone imprint.
All rights reserved. No part of this publication may be reproduced in whole or in part, or
stored in a retrieval system, or transmitted in any form or by any means, electronic, mechanical,
photocopying, recording, or otherwise, without written permission of the publisher.

Editorial Credits
Kristen Mohn, editor; Veronica Scott, designer; Svetlana Zhurkin, media researcher;
Tori Abraham, production specialist

Photo Credits
All photographs by Jeffrey L. Rotman with the exception of:
Asher Gal, 1 (bottom); Dreamstime: Flavijus, 20; Isabelle Delafosse, 3, 40 (right); Shutterstock: Pjard,
6; Sergiy Zavgorodny, 27
Design Elements by Shutterstock

Library of Congress Cataloging-in-Publication Data
Cerullo, Mary M., author.
  Sharks of the deep : a shark photographer's search for sharks at the bottom of the sea /
by Mary M. Cerullo ; photographs by Jeffrey L. Rotman.
    pages cm. — (Compass point books. Shark expedition)
  Summary: "Provides information on deepwater and ocean floor sharks and shares a shark diver's
experiences searching for and photographing them"— Provided by publisher.
  Includes index.
  ISBN 978-0-7565-4886-5 (library binding)
  ISBN 978-0-7565-4909-1 (paperback)
  ISBN 978-0-7565-4913-8 (eBook PDF)
1. Sharks—Juvenile literature. 2. Ocean bottom—Juvenile literature. 3. Rotman, Jeffrey L.—Juvenile
literature. 4. Wildlife photographers—Juvenile literature. 5. Underwater photography—Juvenile
literature. I. Rotman, Jeffrey L., illustrator. II. Title.
  QL638.9.C449 2015
  597.3—dc23   2014009112

For Yair, thanks for giving a voice to my photographs—JLR
To Chris & Taylor, Best Buddies—MMC

Printed in the United States of America in
North Mankato, Minnesota
032014   008087CGF14

TABLE OF CONTENTS

LIVING SCULPTURES

Jeffrey Rotman's career as an underwater photographer drives him to get as close as he can to every sea creature he meets. That brings him face-to-face with many fish—including sharks—and he loves it.

Why sharks, people may ask? "Sharks get such bad press," Jeff replies. "Everyone concentrates on the few big ones that occasionally mistake a human for a seal. You have to look at sharks differently. I see them as living sculptures, especially the bottom sharks and their relatives, the skates and rays. They have an incredible variety of faces, jaws, and shapes. These ocean floor fishes haven't gotten the attention they deserve."

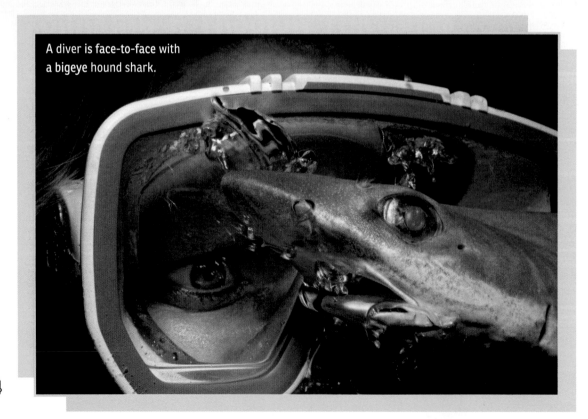
A diver is face-to-face with a bigeye hound shark.

TOP 10 REASONS JEFF LOVES TO DIVE:

1. Meeting cool fish— especially sharks

2. Meeting cool scientists and watching how they work

3. Traveling the world

4. Becoming part of another world

5. Finding something the whole family can do together (if you're Jeff's family!)

6. Making friends for life with dive companions

7. Using really cool (though expensive) equipment

8. Learning valuable lessons— such as don't step on a panther torpedo ray

9. Learning how to become like a fish

10. Using photography and diving skills to help protect sharks, rays, and other ocean life

5

WHERE IT ALL BEGAN

Even though Jeff Rotman has swum in nearly every ocean in the world, the coast of Cape Ann, Massachusetts, is still one of his favorite underwater habitats. It's where he made his first ocean dive.

It was no easy task. Jeff and his dive companion had to scramble over rocks and through crashing waves just to get to the water. They wore wetsuits, weight belts, face masks, fins, and three-fingered gloves called lobster claws to keep their hands warm in the chilly water.

One thing he was not wearing was a scuba tank. Jeff learned to free dive first—a more athletic sport, he feels, than diving with an air supply. He plunged to about 25 feet (7.6 meters) and stayed down for a minute before returning to the surface for air.

As you dive deeper into the water, the temperature also drops—to about 40 degrees Fahrenheit (4.5 degrees Celsius). "When you dive beneath the surface here, the water is green, dark, and cold. There is almost zero visibility," Jeff says. "Once you learn to dive in those conditions, you can dive anywhere." And Jeff has.

Cape Ann, Massachusetts

FREE DIVING

Over time, as Jeff got better at free diving, he was able to stay down for two minutes or even longer. His advice: First, you must be very comfortable in the water. (Jeff even uses yoga breathing exercises to help him relax.) Then you train to hold your breath through lots of practice. He recommends practicing in a swimming pool and swimming laps underwater. Jeff also suggests other sports, such as running, to make you physically fit, because free diving is an extremely demanding activity.

Jeff's son Matthew with a lobster near Cape Ann

yellowtail flounder

FACT:

Because the water is so cold and murky, fewer people dive in New England than in clear tropical seas. But they miss meeting some fascinating creatures lurking in these waters, such as flounder, lobsters, goosefish, and striped bass.

Eventually Jeff started using a scuba tank so he could go deeper—as far as 100 feet (30 m) down. There he poked among the kelp beds, discovering creatures such as sea ravens, wolf eels, sea stars, horseshoe crabs, and giant sea anemones. He learned from field guides, fishermen, and other divers that there were many sharks in these waters, especially small dogfish sharks that often travel in huge schools. Yet they never allowed Jeff to spot them.

The sand tiger shark gets its name from trolling the sand near the ocean floor, hunting for prey.

The only sharks Jeff encountered were the ones swimming in the Giant Ocean Tank at the New England Aquarium in Boston. There he joined staff divers to feed fearsome-looking sand tiger sharks by hand. Long, sharp teeth that stuck out beyond their jaws made them aquarium favorites. But looks can be deceiving. Jeff discovered that sand tiger sharks are quite easygoing in captivity.

After swimming with the sand tigers, Jeff was more determined than ever to meet a shark in the wild.

SAND TIGER SHARK STATS

AVERAGE LENGTH:
6.5 to 9 feet (2 to 2.7 m)

APPROXIMATE WEIGHT:
200 to 300 pounds (91 to 136 kilograms)

RANGE:
worldwide, near the ocean floor

DIET:
mostly bony fish, skates, and other sharks

DIVING THE RED SEA
HAMMERHEADS AND STINGRAYS

Jeff once asked the famous underwater explorer Jacques Cousteau to name his favorite place to dive. "My happiest hours have been spent beneath the waters of the Red Sea," Cousteau replied. It became one of Jeff's favorite places too. In fact, it was there that Jeff met his first shark outside of an aquarium.

It was a scalloped hammerhead—actually, three of them together. They were curious and came within 20 feet (6 m) to check Jeff out. It was a frightening experience, because at the time, all hammerheads had the reputation of being man-eaters. (We now know that is false—only the great hammerhead is dangerous.) So when Jeff saw not just one, but three huge hammerheads coming toward him, his heart started to race. And because things are magnified underwater, they looked even bigger than they were!

The slight curves along the front of the scalloped hammerhead's face help distinguish it from the great hammerhead.

10

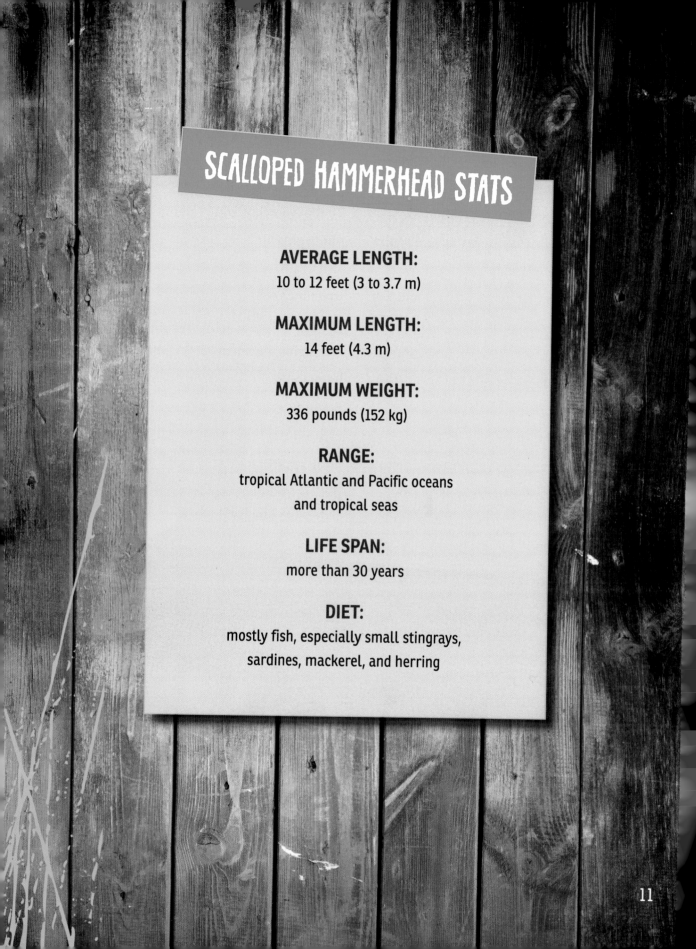

SCALLOPED HAMMERHEAD STATS

AVERAGE LENGTH:
10 to 12 feet (3 to 3.7 m)

MAXIMUM LENGTH:
14 feet (4.3 m)

MAXIMUM WEIGHT:
336 pounds (152 kg)

RANGE:
tropical Atlantic and Pacific oceans
and tropical seas

LIFE SPAN:
more than 30 years

DIET:
mostly fish, especially small stingrays,
sardines, mackerel, and herring

Jeff returns to the Red Sea every year to see the sharks and to dive with two of his children, Adam and Dana, who love the Red Sea as much as he does. Jeff taught all his children to free dive when they were each about 5 years old. Eventually they began to use scuba gear as well.

The Rotman kids learned at an early age which sea creatures they could approach and which were dangerous. They knew that a stingray's venomous spine could inject venom if another animal tried to attack it. They also knew that the stingray only uses its spine to defend itself. As long as the stingray isn't bothered, it should have no need to use its stinger.

When Jeff's son Adam was 11, he came upon a blue-spotted stingray as he was free diving in about 20 feet (6 m) of water. Being a good photographer's son, Adam dove again and again, getting to within inches of the dangerous ray, to make sure his dad got the photo he wanted. The blue-spotted ray did not try to bury itself in the sand as many stingrays do. In fact, it stood its ground as Adam came closer and closer until finally, after several minutes, it got tired of posing and fluttered away.

Jeff's son Adam poses with a blue-spotted stingray

BLUE-SPOTTED STINGRAY STATS

MAXIMUM DISC WIDTH:
14 inches (36 centimeters)

AVERAGE WEIGHT:
11 pounds (5 kg)

RANGE:
tropical Indian and western Pacific oceans, in coral reefs or nearby sandy shallows; rarely found deeper than 100 feet (30 m)

DIET:
snails, clams, crabs, worms, and shrimp

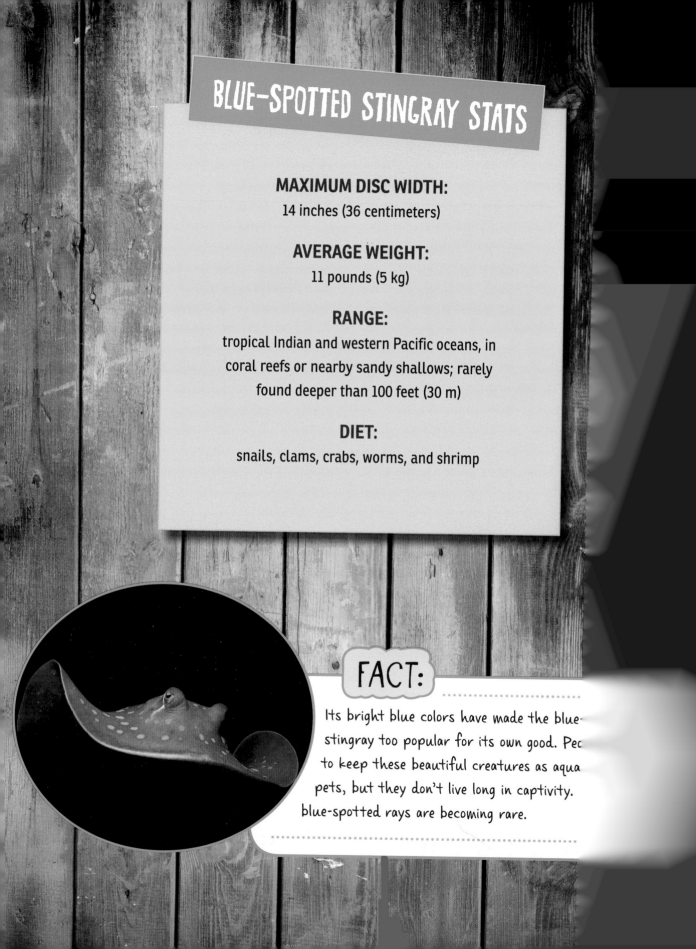

FACT:

Its bright blue colors have made the blue-stingray too popular for its own good. Pec to keep these beautiful creatures as aqua pets, but they don't live long in captivity. blue-spotted rays are becoming rare.

Rays and skates are members of a special branch of the shark family. Scientists estimate that there are about 500 kinds of rays. They range from the short-nose electric ray, which is about the size and shape of a pancake, to the magnificent manta ray, which can grow to be more than 20 feet (6 m) across.

In shallow water stingrays can present a problem to beachgoers. Tourists walking along the shores of the Red Sea are warned to shuffle their feet to scare up hidden rays.

manta ray, the largest of rays

A panther torpedo ray uses camouflage to hide in the sand, ready to surprise prey.

Jeff forgot that lesson one time and stepped on a panther torpedo ray. He got a shock from the electric ray that nearly knocked him off his feet. Some bottom sharks and rays can generate a strong electrical discharge to stun prey or predators. A shock can deliver up to 200 volts—nearly twice the voltage of a typical household electrical outlet. "And once you get such a shock—whether you're human or fish—you remember it!" Jeff says.

MADE FOR LIFE AT THE BOTTOM

Imagine squashing a shark so flat that it would fit against the ocean bottom. In a way, that is what nature has done with the ray and its relatives, which evolved from sharks.

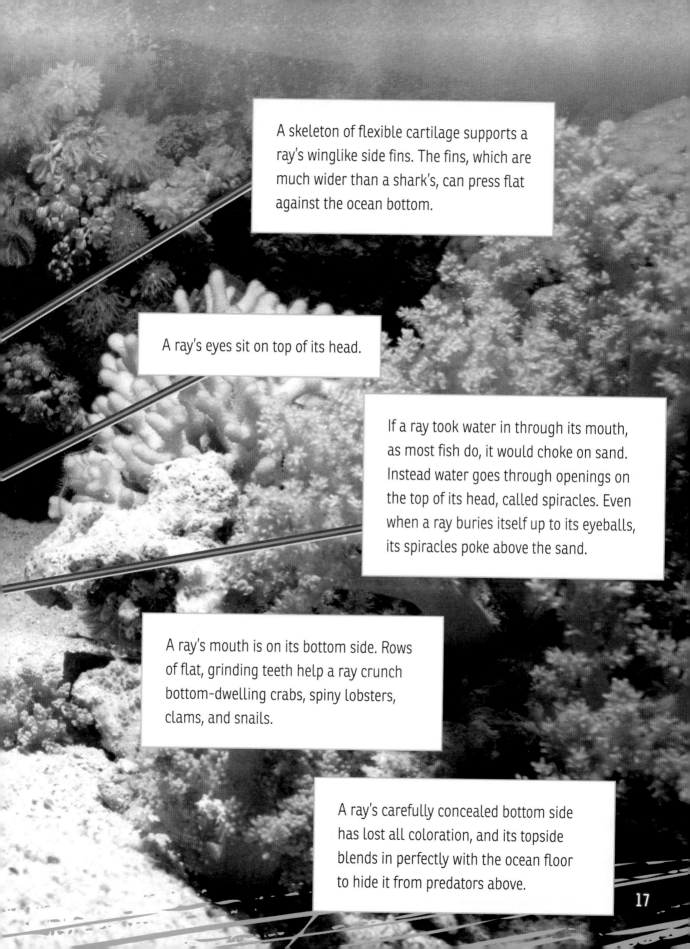

A skeleton of flexible cartilage supports a ray's winglike side fins. The fins, which are much wider than a shark's, can press flat against the ocean bottom.

A ray's eyes sit on top of its head.

If a ray took water in through its mouth, as most fish do, it would choke on sand. Instead water goes through openings on the top of its head, called spiracles. Even when a ray buries itself up to its eyeballs, its spiracles poke above the sand.

A ray's mouth is on its bottom side. Rows of flat, grinding teeth help a ray crunch bottom-dwelling crabs, spiny lobsters, clams, and snails.

A ray's carefully concealed bottom side has lost all coloration, and its topside blends in perfectly with the ocean floor to hide it from predators above.

LOOKING DEEPER
PYGMY AND HOUND SHARKS

To learn more about deepwater sharks and other creatures, Jeff joined an expedition of ocean scientists from Eilat, Israel, who were studying the marine life in the depths of the Red Sea. Their equipment could go much deeper than a human diver ever could.

The researchers lowered baited fishing lines and barbless hooks to the ocean floor, more than a half-mile below the surface. After many hours they raised the lines very slowly, so that deep-sea creatures used to living under extreme pressure could adjust to the lesser pressure at the surface. Jeff was one of the first people to meet—and photograph—the rare Moses smoothhound shark and the bigeye hound shark. The name bigeye fits—the deepwater sharks have huge eyes to pick up any faint light that glimmers from other deep-sea animals. Since they mostly feed on bottom creatures, having their mouth underneath allows them to easily graze for food on the ocean floor.

Moses smoothhound shark

THE PRESSURE IS ON

The deeper you dive into the ocean, the greater the pressure you feel from the weight of the water above you. At a depth of 3,000 feet (914 m), the water pressure is enough to squeeze a piece of wood to half its size. Even the most experienced scuba divers can only dive to about 300 feet (91 m) before the water pressure becomes too much.

bigeye hound shark

The bigeye hound shark is part of the hound shark family. There are about 30 species of hound sharks.

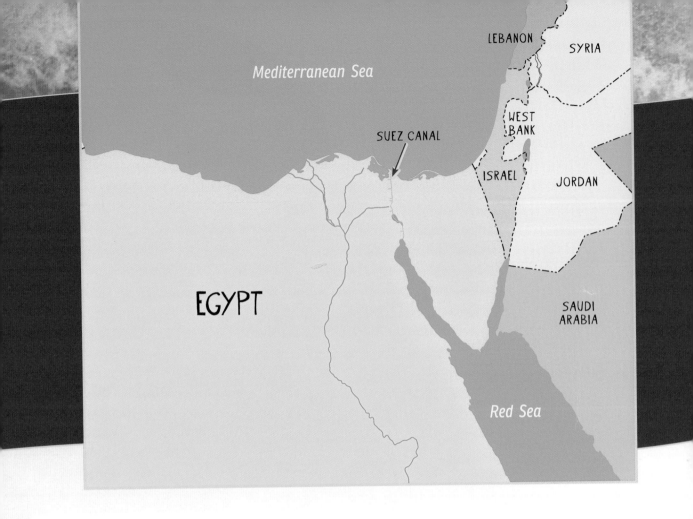

Jeff also went to sea with scientists from the University of Haifa in Israel to explore the bottom of the Mediterranean Sea on the other side of the Suez Canal from the Red Sea. Their nets pulled up a strange sea creature from a depth of 3,000 feet (914 m). Rows of tiny light organs on its belly emitted a faint glow, like a firefly. Perhaps these lights were meant to attract the attention of unsuspecting prey in the deep ocean. The fish had huge eyes, likely used to see prey such as squid and other fish that also produce their own living light. Imagine how bright the sun must have seemed to a "lightning bug" from the bottom of the sea.

The exotic specimen was a spined pygmy shark, about 8 inches (20 cm) long. Although it is one of the smallest sharks in the world, it ranks as the top predator in the ocean food chain of the deep Mediterranean.

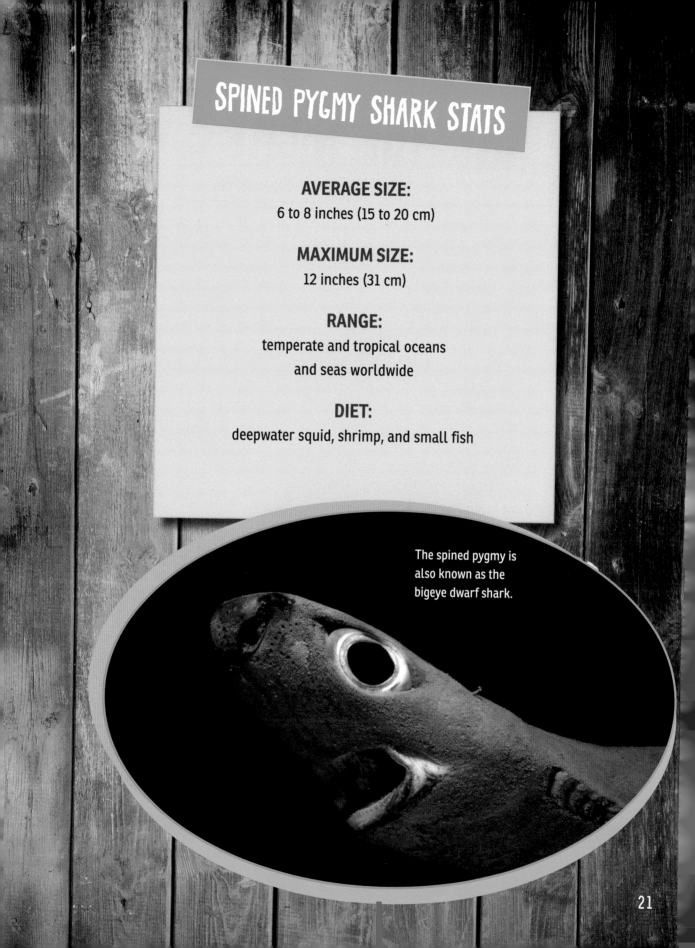

SPINED PYGMY SHARK STATS

AVERAGE SIZE:
6 to 8 inches (15 to 20 cm)

MAXIMUM SIZE:
12 inches (31 cm)

RANGE:
temperate and tropical oceans
and seas worldwide

DIET:
deepwater squid, shrimp, and small fish

The spined pygmy is
also known as the
bigeye dwarf shark.

WORKING THE NIGHT SHIFT

NURSE SHARKS

When Jeff Rotman goes to the islands, he doesn't hang out on the beach like the sunbathers do. He heads straight for more interesting stretches of sand beneath the ocean. There he meets the most engaging creatures. On a trip to the Bahamas, Jeff made friends with a "local"—a nurse shark.

The nurse shark didn't seem to mind Jeff's company, possibly because nurse sharks often gather in groups. Sometimes they even sit on top of one another, creating big piles of nurse sharks. Or perhaps the nurse shark was more interested in napping. While many sharks have to keep moving to push enough water over their gills to breathe, a nurse shark can pump water over its gills as it lays motionless on the ocean floor.

Like many bottom sharks and rays, the nurse shark is nocturnal. During the day it rests on the ocean floor, only springing into action if an unsuspecting crab or snail wanders too close to resist. At night a nurse shark rouses itself to actively hunt for food.

A nurse shark has barbels, which are two pieces of skin that hang from its upper jaw like a droopy moustache. These barbels can feel and taste, to help the shark find food in the sand as it cruises along the ocean floor.

A nurse shark can also vacuum up its prey. It cups its mouth over the opening of a small cave or crevice and sucks out a tasty crab or octopus. It's even been known to yank snails right out of their shells.

Nurse sharks tend to ignore humans, but a diver who accidentally steps on one may get a bite from the shark's tiny but strong teeth.

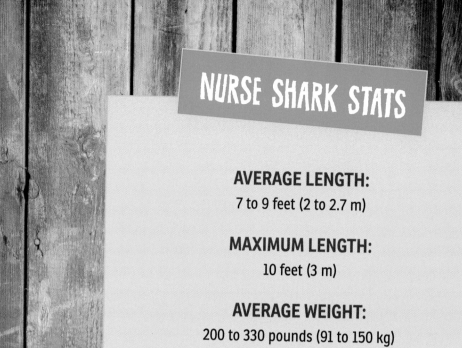

NURSE SHARK STATS

AVERAGE LENGTH:
7 to 9 feet (2 to 2.7 m)

MAXIMUM LENGTH:
10 feet (3 m)

AVERAGE WEIGHT:
200 to 330 pounds (91 to 150 kg)

RANGE:
Atlantic coast from Carolinas to Florida Keys,
Gulf of Mexico, and Caribbean

DIET:
crabs, shrimp, squid, and small fish

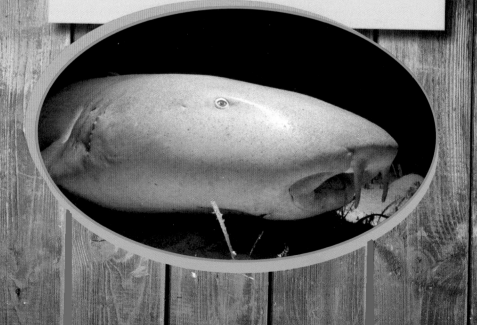

STINGRAY CITY

One of Jeff's oldest friends is Neal Watson. Neal runs dive resorts throughout the Caribbean. Neal was the first scuba diver to reach a depth of 437 feet (133 m), which put him into the *Guinness Book of World Records*.

Neal and his two sons, Neal Jr., 12, and John, 13, planned a trip to the Cayman Islands to swim with stingrays. Neal invited Jeff to come along and to bring his camera. Jeff arrived at the airport with eight large suitcases filled with photographic equipment, dive gear, and two bathing suits.

Together they flew to a string of islands in the western Caribbean Sea. Near the largest island, Grand Cayman, is a lagoon where local fishermen come to clean their catch after a day of fishing. They dump the unwanted fish parts overboard into the shallow bay. Southern stingrays discovered this free food and started showing up regularly. Soon the bay became known as Stingray City.

southern stingray

A SHARK PHOTOGRAPHER'S PACKING LIST

Dive Gear:

several wet suits of varying thicknesses, two masks, a snorkel, a buoyancy compensator vest, weight belt with weights, and fins

Camera Gear:

dive lights, eight cameras, three camera housings to protect cameras from the water, four strobes for underwater flash to restore the natural color, and various camera lenses

Safety Gear:

a compass, a depth gauge, a dive knife, a safety orange strobe for night dives, and a safety sausage tube to wave at the surface in case of separation from the dive boat

Onboard Equipment:

a laptop to download photos from the camera, back-up equipment for everything, including extra batteries for cameras and strobes, and a few good books to read between dives

Every morning dozens of stingrays visit the lagoon to take handouts of squid from tourist divers. The rays swim from dive boat to dive boat, like trick-or-treaters going door-to-door, begging for candy. The stingrays eagerly crowd around each diver, waiting for their treat. Although tourists are warned to watch out for the venomous spines of the stingrays, the animals only use them for defense, never to attack. While most rays move on after getting a piece of squid, some stingrays play tricks to get even more. One stingray knocked off a diver's mask, making her drop her bag of bait in surprise. As if on cue, another ray rushed in to gobble up the goodies!

To make sure they would get good photographs of the stingrays with the boys, Jeff and Neal stuffed handfuls of squid inside the pockets of the boys' dive vests. But the delicious smell sent the stingrays into a feeding frenzy once the boys hit the water. The overexcited rays dive-bombed them to try to get at the food. The boys quickly retreated to the boat and dug the squid out of their vests. They decided to take a different approach.

Back underwater, they held out pieces of squid in their hands. Now the stingrays approached more politely. The boys spent the next several hours happily petting and playing with the stingrays, lifting them from underneath to avoid the venomous spines.

The Watsons dive with stingrays.

SOUTHERN STINGRAY STATS

AVERAGE SIZE:
females 4 feet (1.2 m),
males 2 to 3 feet
(61 to 91 cm) across

MAXIMUM WIDTH:
5 feet (1.5 m)

RANGE:
Atlantic Ocean, from New Jersey
to Brazil, throughout Caribbean

DIET:
mollusks, worms, shrimp,
crabs, and small fish

JEFF'S SHARK CLOSE-UPS FROM AROUND THE (BOTTOM OF THE) WORLD

EASTERN FIDDLER RAY:

sometimes called banjo sharks, fiddlers are members of the shovelnose group of rays

ZEBRA SHARK:

once it reaches adulthood, small dots replace its stripes

SPOTTED EAGLE RAY:

able to leap completely out of the water to escape a predator

WOBBEGONG SHARK:

may look lazy and harmless, but if you don't treat it with respect, it will grab onto you with its powerful jaws and not let go

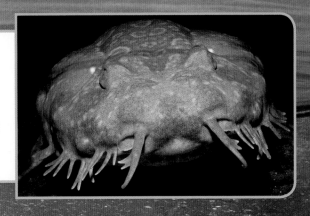

PORT JACKSON SHARK:

sports a spine on its dorsal fin, which it stabs into any predator that tries to swallow it

EPAULETTE SHARK:

like a badge on a military uniform, the shark has a big black oval on its shoulder that would-be predators may mistake for a giant eye

CALIFORNIA HORN SHARK:

has a powerful sense of smell, thanks to many folds of skin inside its nostrils

A NEW GENERATION OF DIVERS

Jeff often returns to his favorite place off Cape Ann, Massachusetts, to share its mysteries with his younger sons Matthew and Thomas. Like their dad, the boys are skilled divers. And like their dad, they feel at home in the rough, chilly waters of the North Atlantic Ocean. They are even better than their father at spying animals camouflaged against sand and seaweed, such as lobsters, moon snails, and bottom fish.

On one dive the spiracles of a little skate buried in the coarse sandy bottom caught the boys' eagle-eyed attention. They watched it for a while, but it wasn't until Thomas reached down to grab the skate that it finally tried to escape. Thomas was too quick, though, and caught it by its tail. He knew that skates don't have a venomous spine at the base of their tail like most stingrays.

Flapping its wings as hard as it could, the little skate swiveled its eyes around to see what creature had seized it. Thomas gently turned the skate over, and both boys took turns running their gloved fingers over the rows of small teeth that munch on crabs, sea urchins, and squid.

Thomas swimming with the skate

LITTLE SKATE STATS

AVERAGE SIZE:
16 to 20 inches (41 to 51 cm)

MAXIMUM SIZE:
21 inches (53 cm)

MAXIMUM WEIGHT:
1.5 to 2 pounds (680 to 907 grams)

RANGE:
Atlantic coast of North America
from Nova Scotia to Virginia

LIFE SPAN:
about 14 years

DIET:
hermit crabs, other crabs,
squid, worms, and small fish

Jeff's boys sometimes find old skate
egg cases on the beach and bring
them home as souvenirs.

Because many rays and bottom sharks live near coastlines where humans also like to visit, there are bound to be accidental encounters between the species. But many aquariums actually encourage humans and rays to interact by providing opportunities to pet these flattened sharks.

At the New England Aquarium in Boston, Massachusetts, visitors can gently stroke cownose rays, Atlantic rays, and epaulette sharks as they glide around a shallow pool that recreates a coastal mangrove. The exhibit explains how stingrays are important parts of the ocean food web, feeding on other bottom dwellers such as clams, crabs, and small fish. Rays are favorite meals for many kinds of sharks.

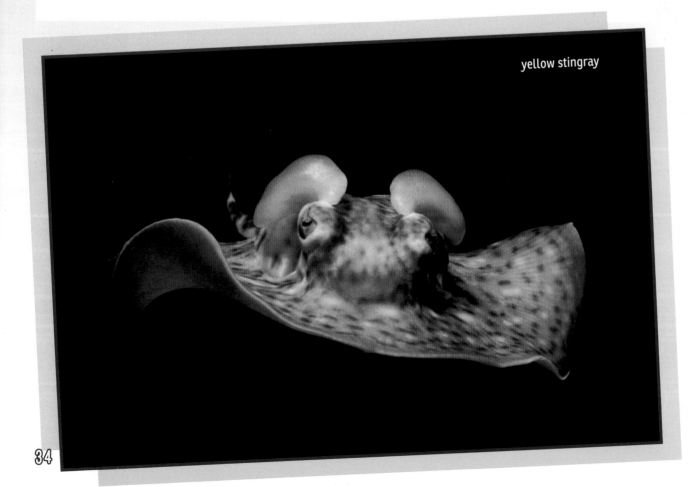

yellow stingray

southern stingray

But aquarium exhibit designers most want people to appreciate the adaptations that make these sharks so unique: their shapes, skin patterns, and behavior. Once a stingray comes to the surface and allows you to pet it, you will never feel afraid of one again.

SHARING A PASSION FOR SHARKS

"The ocean is a bridge between my children and me," Jeff says. "Diving is a shared experience that takes us away from our everyday world. It's also a connection with my dive friends and the people I meet who are working to protect sharks and other sea creatures."

Jeff believes in sharing his passion with everyone he can. His photography is another bridge—one between sea animals and humans, providing us a glimpse of the wonders found underwater. The better we understand and appreciate what's below, the better we can help ensure that deep-sea creatures will be swimming far into the future.

GLOSSARY

barbel—a whiskerlike feeler on the jaws of some fish

buoyancy compensator vest—a piece of diving equipment that controls buoyancy by inflating or deflating a bladder with gas from the air tank or diver's mouth

cartilage—a strong, rubbery tissue that connects bones in people and animals; in sharks, the entire skeleton is composed of cartilage rather than bone

free diving—to swim underwater without scuba equipment and while holding your breath

gill—a body part on the side of a fish; fish use their gills to breathe

kelp—a large, brown algae with long fronds, the seaweed version of leaves

mangrove—a tree that grows in large clumps at the water's edge in warm seas, creating a shelter and nursery ground for many marine animals

nocturnal—active at night and resting during the day

scuba—self-contained underwater breathing apparatus, based on the device developed by Emile Gagnan and Jacques Cousteau, which uses a tank of compressed gas (usually air) for diving

skate—a member of the ray family that doesn't have a venomous spine at the base of its tail; it relies on spiky projections on its back and tail to discourage predators

spiracles—small holes through which some animals breathe

READ MORE

Discovery Channel. *The Big Book of Sharks.*
New York: Time Home Entertainment, 2012.

Disney Book Group. *Wonderful World of Sharks.*
New York: Disney Press, 2012.

Zieger, Jennifer. *Stingrays.*
New York: Children's Press, 2012.

INTERNET SITES

Use FactHound to find Internet sites related to this book.
All of the sites on FactHound have been researched by our staff.

Here's all you do:

Visit *www.facthound.com*

Type in this code:
9780756548865

AUTHOR

Mary M. Cerullo has been teaching and writing about the ocean and natural history for 40 years. She has written more than 20 children's books on ocean life. Mary is also associate director of the conservation organization Friends of Casco Bay/Casco Baykeeper in Maine, where she lives with her family.

Mary with granddaughter Taylor

PHOTOGRAPHER

Jeffrey L. Rotman is one of the world's leading underwater photographers. Diving and shooting for more than 40 years—and in nearly every ocean and sea in the world—this Boston native combines an artist's eye with a naturalist's knowledge of his subjects. His photography has been featured on television and in print worldwide. Jeff and his family live in New Jersey.

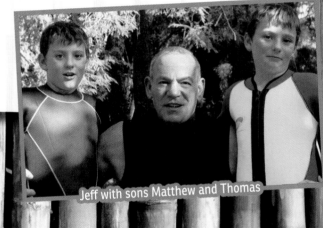
Jeff with sons Matthew and Thomas

INDEX

BEACH
50m

SURF

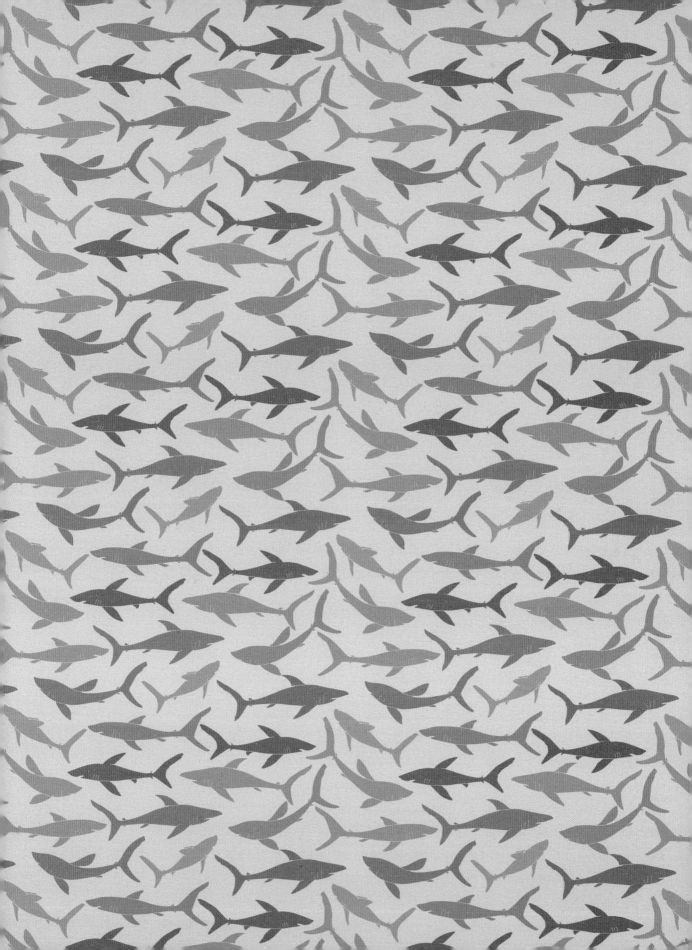